DISNEP

Tangled

Adapted by
Ben Smiley

Illustrated by
Victoria Ying

g **A GOLDEN BOOK • NEW YORK**

www.randomhouse.com/kids

ISBN: 978-0-7364-2684-8

Printed in the United States of America

2019 18 17 16 15 14

Rapunzel had long, long, long hair and lived in a tall, tall tower. Her hair was as long as the tower was tall. When Mother Gothel came home every day, she called, **"Rapunzel, let down your hair!"** And Rapunzel pulled Mother Gothel up into the tower.

Rapunzel's hair was **magical**. It kept Mother Gothel young and beautiful.

Rapunzel did not know that Mother Gothel had stolen her from her real parents, the King and the Queen.

Mother Gothel wanted the **magical** hair all for herself.

Mother Gothel never let Rapunzel leave the tower. She told Rapunzel that bad people wanted to take her **magical** hair. Rapunzel had one friend—a chameleon named **Pascal**.

Once a year, on her birthday, Rapunzel saw **sparkling lights** floating into the sky. She wished she could leave the tower and see the lights up close. They seemed **meant** for her.

One day, just before Rapunzel's eighteenth birthday, a thief named **Flynn** was running through the forest. He had stolen the lost princess's crown. While trying to get away from Maximus, a determined horse from the royal guard, Flynn found Rapunzel's hidden tower.

Flynn climbed up the tower to hide. Rapunzel had never seen another person besides Mother Gothel. Rapunzel thought Flynn wanted her hair. But he didn't. Rapunzel showed Flynn a painting she had made of the **lights** and asked him to take her to see them. Flynn agreed.

On the way, Flynn and Rapunzel stopped in a pub. It was filled with scary-looking men. But they didn't want to steal Rapunzel's hair, either. They were **friendly.**

Maximus and some royal guards found Flynn. One of the scary-looking men helped Flynn and Rapunzel escape.

They ran until they got trapped in a water-filled cave. Rapunzel's magical **glowing** hair helped them find a way out!

But Maximus found Flynn again. The horse wanted to take Flynn to jail. Rapunzel told **Maximus** it was her birthday. She asked him to let Flynn take her to see the sparkling lights. Maximus agreed. Rapunzel's wish was about to come true!

Flynn and Rapunzel had a **wonderful** day. A little boy gave Rapunzel a small kingdom flag. The kingdom was celebrating the birthday of the lost princess.

The lost princess had the same birthday as Rapunzel!

Rapunzel saw a picture of the King and the Queen holding their baby princess. The Queen and the Princess had **green eyes**—just like Rapunzel!

Suddenly, Rapunzel was swept up in a dance! It was the most **fun** she had ever had . . . so far.

That night, the people of the kingdom lit lanterns. At last, Rapunzel's wish came true. Overjoyed, she saw the **sparkling lights** fill the sky. She loved the world outside the tower. She loved Flynn. And he loved her, too.

On shore, Flynn left Rapunzel and did not return. Rapunzel was **heartbroken**. She did not know that Flynn had been tricked by evil Mother Gothel. He had been captured and put in jail! Mother Gothel found Rapunzel and took her back to the tower.

Back in her room, Rapunzel realized that she had been painting the kingdom's emblem, the **golden sun**, on her wall her entire life!

Rapunzel remembered the picture of the **lost princess** and the Queen. Now Rapunzel knew why they all looked alike.

Mother Gothel was the only one who wanted to steal Rapunzel's **magical** hair. She had lied to Rapunzel about everything. **"Mother, I am the lost princess,"** Rapunzel said.

Meanwhile, Flynn had escaped and arrived at the tower to rescue Rapunzel. **"Rapunzel! Rapunzel! Let down your hair!"** he called.

But Mother Gothel would not let Rapunzel go. Mother Gothel hurt Flynn so badly that he could never, ever take Rapunzel from her.

Flynn still thought of a way to save Rapunzel. He **cut** her hair. Without Rapunzel's magical hair, Mother Gothel withered away. Rapunzel was finally free of the evil woman.

But without her long hair, Rapunzel had no more magic to save Flynn. He closed his eyes for the last time. Rapunzel cried. A single **golden tear** fell on Flynn's cheek. It contained the last bit of magic left inside Rapunzel. Flynn's eyes opened! He was all right!

Rapunzel went to her real parents, the King and the Queen. After eighleen years of waiting, they took one look at the **green-eyed** girl and knew she was their daughter. Rapunzel had come home at last!

Rapunzel loved her new life. She loved the world outside the tower. She loved her new friends. At last, she knew where she belonged.

And they all lived **happily** ever after.